in TROUBLE is a GIRLS BEST FRIEND!

BEANObooks

published under licence by

meadowside
CHILDREN'S BOOKS

BAD DAD

Minnie kicked the garden gate open and stomped up the path.

"Temper, temper!" said Mum as she opened the front door.

"I'm bored!" said Minnie with a scowl. "I'm bored and skint, as usual!"

"When I was young, we used to play with sticks and stones and think ourselves lucky!" said Mum.

"When I was young, we used to do chores like washing cars to earn money," Dad added.

"I didn't think they had cars when you were young," Minnie retorted. Dad shook his fist at her, but Minnie didn't notice. Dad had given her an idea.

"Maybe I could do a few easy chores for a bit of dosh," Minnie thought to herself. "Not car washing – that's too much like hard work! Hmmm…"

Five minutes later Minnie had designed a big poster. She went out to the street and stuck it to the lamppost.

Minnie stepped back to admire her poster and trod on her next-door neighbour's foot.

"YOWeEEee!"

yelled Mrs Richards, hopping around. "Minnie, why do you have to be such a minx? I'm going away for the weekend and I still have so much to sort out! And now I have to do it with a limp!"

Minnie noticed that Mrs Richards was carrying a suitcase.

"Do you need any easy jobs doing while you're away?" asked Minnie.

She pointed at the poster.

"Well," said Mrs Richards, "I have been worrying about my darling plants. I would like someone to water them while I'm away."

"Hmm," said Minnie. "Watering plants doesn't sound like hard work!"

"Oh no!" said Mrs Richards. "Just a little bit of water will do."

Mrs Richards gave Minnie her spare house key.

"Not too much water, remember!" she said. "Just a few drops every day!"

She waved goodbye and drove off. A smile spread slowly over Minnie's face.

"Easy dosh!" she grinned. "How hard can it be to water a few plants?"

After Mrs Richards left, Minnie had a brainwave.

"What's the point of going back every day when I could give the plants enough water for the whole week all at once?" she thought. "That will give me more time for minxing!"

Minnie let herself into Mrs Richard's house. As she opened the door, she noticed a hose coiled up by the back door.

"Hmm," said Minnie. "I'm having another brainwave!"

Minnie picked up the hose and attached it to the kitchen tap.

"Another timesaver!" she grinned. "This will be much faster than filling up a stupid watering can every two minutes!"

First Minnie went into the sitting room. Plants were everywhere. There were weeping figs on the windowsill and busy lizzies on the bookcase. There were spider plants on the shelves and cacti on the coffee table.

"Mad," muttered Minnie. She turned on the hose and squirted water into the plant pots, filling them right up to make sure they had enough. It only took a few minutes to water all the plants in the sitting room.

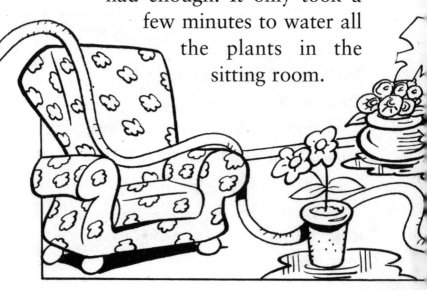

"Easy job!" Minnie smirked. She turned off the hose and walked upstairs, pulling the hose behind her.

But the hose wasn't quite long enough. As Minnie walked upstairs, the hose came off the kitchen tap with a loud

POP!

Upstairs, Minnie found even more plants. There were begonias in the bedroom and lilies on the landing. Minnie turned on the hose, but there was only a dribble of water.

"Come on!" ordered Minnie, shaking the hose. But no water came out.

"WORK!" Minnie raged, stamping on the hose.

It was no good – there was no water.

"Huh, rubbish thing," huffed Minnie, stamping downstairs. "I'll just have to use the stupid watering can after all."

She raced downstairs and jumped down the last three steps.

The whole of the downstairs was covered in water!

Minnie ran into the kitchen and turned off the tap. She filled the watering can from a puddle by the fridge and went upstairs to water the plants. Then she locked up the house and left Mrs Richard's key under her mat.

"That's a good job done!" said Minnie, rubbing her hands together in glee. "The water's bound to disappear before Mrs Richards gets back. Now all I have to do is wait for Mrs Richards to come home and collect my dosh!"

On Sunday evening there was a loud knock on the door. It was Mrs Richards. Her face was a very funny colour and when she saw Minnie she started to steam.

"Have you come to pay me?" asked Minnie.

"PAY YOU?"

shouted Mrs Richards. "My house is flooded and all my plants are dead from overwatering! You're going to pay me!"

"What's all this about?" asked Dad.

"Huh," said Minnie. "You had too many plants anyway!"

Dad sighed and pulled out his chequebook as Minnie raced out of the house.

Outside, Minnie bumped into Soppy Susan, who had a small poodle on a lead.

"Get outta my way!" growled Minnie.

"Leave me alone," said Susan. "I'm walking my uncle's dog and we're going to the park."

Susan skipped off and Minnie stared after her.

"Dog walking!" she said. "There are loads of people with big fat pets who need exercise! But I'm not gonna walk just one dog – I'm gonna walk more dogs than anyone else!"

Minnie quickly stuck up a sign.

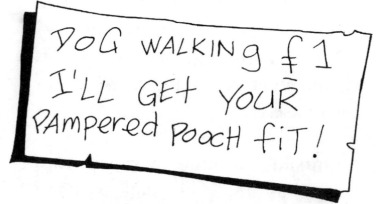

Soon Minnie had twenty-three customers. They all paid her and then handed over their dogs.

"Come back here in one hour to collect them," said Minnie as they hurried off. She rattled the coins in her pocket and looked at the dogs.

There were dogs of ever size, colour and breed. There were good dogs and bad dogs. There were loud dogs and quiet dogs.

"Come on, you mutts, we're going to the park," said Minnie.

"WALKIES!"

The dogs leapt into the air and started to run. Minnie raced along behind them, holding on to the leads with all her might.

The dogs were tough and determined, but so was Minnie. No matter what they did to shake her off, she hung grimly on to their leads as they raced towards the park.

"Right, you horrible hounds!" Minnie yelled, digging in her heels and grinding the dogs to a halt. "We're gonna go down by the pond – and the ice cream van!"

She rattled her coins again and licked her lips. But before she could turn left to go the pond, she felt all the leads go stiff.

The dogs were suddenly silent, staring at a tiny dot that was walking towards them through the park. Minnie strained her eyes as the dot grew slowly bigger. It was actually two dots… she could see red and black stripes… wiry black hair…

"Oh, it's only the Menace," realised Minnie.

"… and Gnasher!" howled the twenty three dogs in terror. They leapt in every direction to escape from the dreaded tripe hound and there was a loud SNAP as twenty three leads broke at the same time..

"Come back here!" Minnie bellowed, as they flew off in all directions. But it was no use. Minnie was left with a handful of broken leads.

Minnie spent all afternoon combing the park for the dogs, while Dennis and Gnasher chortled at her. But she only managed to find a small Pekinese.

"I'll get you back for this," Minnie growled. She raced out of the park and past her dog walking sign, where the owners were waiting for her.

"HEY, COME BACK HERE!"

they yelled. "Bring back our dogs!"

Minnie threw the pound coins (and the Pekinese) at them and zoomed through Beanotown, through her garden gate, into her house and under the sofa in the sitting room.

"What was that?" asked Dad, who had only seen a blur.

The doorbell rang and Mum went to answer it. Minnie heard the voices of twenty three angry dog owners.

"She's not here," said Mum, not knowing that Minnie was squashed under her best flowery sofa. "Now clear off!"

Mum walked into the sitting room.

"Who was at the door?" asked Dad.

"Oh, something to do with Minnie," said Mum. "Never mind that. I've got something to ask you. It's your birthday tomorrow and you still haven't told me what you want."

Dad gave a loud sigh.

"Just the usual," he said.

"Oh no!" muttered Minnie. "I totally forgot it was Dad's birthday –

and I haven't got any dosh! I can't afford to buy him his usual socks!"

"I don't want a present," sighed Dad, who was feeling very sorry for himself. "I'm getting old! If only I could be a kid again – just for a day!"

"Well, I think you are going to have to settle for aftershave," said Mum.

"Hmm," said Minnie. "I think I'm getting another brilliant idea!"

In the morning, Minnie found Dad slumped sadly over a large bowl of porridge. He had two presents next to him on the kitchen table – a pink tie from Mum and a sink plunger from Uncle Algie.

"Happy birthday, Dad!" said Minnie.

Dad just grunted.

22

"I haven't got you socks this year," said Minnie. "I've got you something really different instead."

Dad began to feel slightly worried.

"It's not another sink plunger, is it?"

"No," grinned Minnie. "It's a whole day of being a kid again."

A small smile crept onto Dad's face. Mum put her hands on her hips.

"What about work?" she asked.

"He's bunking off!" said Minnie, grabbing Dad's hand and pulling him out of the back door before Mum could stop them.

"So what's first?" asked Dad. "I'm a bit rusty at being a kid."

"First, every kid has to know how to fire a catapult," said Minnie. She whipped her best catapult from

under her beret and handed it to Dad. Then she filled up some water bombs from the garden tap.

"Kid Lesson Number One," said Minnie. "Fire a water bomb over the fence into next door's garden and hit the big apple tree."

Dad took careful aim and fired the first water bomb.

"SPLAT!" It hit the fence.
"Try again," Minnie giggled.

Dad took aim a
second time. SPLAT!
He hit Chester!
"SCREeEeECH!"
yowled Chester.

"Sorry, Chester!" called Dad, but
Minnie clapped her hand over his
mouth.

"Never apologise!"
she growled. "Try again!"

Dad took aim
with his third water bomb.
He screwed up his face,
stuck out his tongue to
help him concentrate
and... "SPLAT!"
... Dad's water bomb
exploded on Mum's
head as she was pegging
out the washing!

"Excellent shot!" hooted Minnie.

"My new perm is ruined!" shrieked Mum, marching towards them.

"Scarper, Dad!" Minnie yelled. They raced out of the garden and down the road.

"What's next?" puffed Dad.

"Target practice!" said Minnie. She pulled her peashooter from under her beret and handed it to Dad. Then she set up a row of old tin cans along their neighbour's fence.

"All you have to do is shoot the tin cans off the fence," said Minnie. "Piece of cake!"

Dad nervously put the peashooter to his mouth. He aimed at the cans, crossed his fingers and BLEW!

RAT-A-TAT-RAT-A-TAT!

The pellets flew past the tin cans, into their neighbour's garden and peppered the dog kennel like hail. The dog was startled out of a very happy dream about chasing Chester. He sprang to his feet and saw Dad.

"Er, Dad…" said Minnie.

"I know!" said Dad.

"SCARPER!"

He raced off down the street as fast as he could, and the dog leapt after him, while Minnie doubled up with laughter.

"That's the most exercise Dad's had in years!" she chortled.

The dog chased Dad around Beanotown three times until a sausage delivery at the butcher's distracted it. Dad staggered back home, panting, with sweat pouring down his face. Minnie was waiting for him in the garden.

"What kept you?" she asked.

"I need a rest!" gasped Dad.

"No time for resting when you're a kid," said Minnie firmly. "You've gotta be up and at 'em! Come on!"

Minnie showed Dad what she had made for him. She had attached all the wheeled toys she could find to the back of her bike.

"It's a moving target," she explained. "A modern kid has gotta be able to hit a moving target with a water pistol."

She handed him her best water pistol and hopped onto her bike.

"I'm gonna drag these targets along and you need to hit them all!" she said. "Ready?"

"No!" groaned Dad, wiping his forehead.

Minnie started to pedal. She whizzed around the garden, dragging the convoy of toys behind her, and Dad fired the water pistol at the targets. He missed the tricycle and the hobby horse, but then he gave a yell of triumph.

"Shot!" he bellowed.

"What did you hit?" asked Minnie.

"The toy policeman!" cheered Dad, punching the air.

"But... there isn't a toy policeman!" said Minnie, confused.

Just then the purple face of Sergeant Slipper appeared over the garden fence, without his cap.

"Uh-oh," chortled Minnie, slipping into the bushes.

"Do you know that it's a crime to knock off a policeman's hat?" roared Sergeant Slipper.

"I'm not apologising!" said Dad, remembering what Minnie had told him.

"Is that so?" asked Sergeant Slipper. "In that case... you can come down to the station and explain yourself!"

Dad was marched down to the station and Minnie rolled around the garden in fits of laughter, clutching her stomach.

"Where's Dad?" asked Mum, wondering what all the noise was about.

"He didn't have time to learn the last lesson of being a kid," chortled Minnie. "Never stand still when Sergeant Slipper's heading your way!"

Minnie was just scoffing the last few crumbs of Dad's birthday cake when he came home. She his the empty cake plate behind her back, but Dad gave her a huge smile.

"That's OK, Minnie," he said. "You deserve a treat after the wonderful present you gave me!"

Minnie frowned. What was Dad up to?

"What do you mean?" she asked suspiciously. Dad casually locked the back door.

"You gave me the best birthday present EVER," he told her. "I was feeling sad about my birthday – wishing I was still a kid. But you changed all that!"

He took a step towards her.

"You made me realise that there are lots of advantages to being a dad."

"That's great," said Minnie, edging around the kitchen table.

"I can drive a car..."

He took another step towards her...

"... I don't have to go to school..."

He took a third step in her direction...

"... but best of all..."

He grabbed her by the collar...

"... I CAN SEND YOU TO YOUR ROOM!"

Minnie was propelled upstairs in a rage and Mum gave a snort of laughter.

"Minnie may be a minx," she chuckled, "but today you've been a thoroughly bad dad!"

FRIGHT FARM

Minnie's class was going on a trip to a local farm.

"I don't want to go!" grumbled Minnie. She stuck out her lip and frowned.

"Everyone has to go," said Dad, trying to push her onto the school bus. "No arguments!"

"Who cares about stupid farms anyway?" Minnie fumed, hanging on to the sides of the bus to stop him pushing her on board.

"You will, by the time this trip is over!" yelled Dad. "You're going to have good time whether you like it or not!"

He gave a final shove and pushed Minnie onto the first step of the bus.

"You need to learn about Mother Nature!" he said.

"I'm not interested in stupid Mother Nature!" Minnie roared. "I'm interested in minxing!"

Dad rolled his eyes at Mr McDonald, Minnie's teacher, who was sitting at the steering wheel, gripping it very tightly.

"Just do your best, Mr McDonald," said Dad.

Mr McDonald gave a low groan.

Minnie stomped onto the bus and cleared the back seat with a couple of well-aimed shots from her catapult.

"Grrr," moaned Plug, pulling a dried pea out of his ear. "Does she have to come?"

"No," said Minnie.

"Yes," said Mr McDonald, starting the engine. "Now BEHAVE, you lot!"

"Yeah right," muttered Minnie under her breath.

"Oh, this will be so much fun!" simpered Soppy Susan, clasping her hands together. "I love animals!"

"Are you sure?" said Minnie. A minxing grin spread over her face. "Farms are pretty mucky places you know. Do you really want to get manure all over your pretty little shoes?"

Soppy Susan's lips started to tremble.

"M-m-manure?" she stammered.

"And then there's the straw that'll get stuck in your hair and the pong that'll hang around for days," Minnie added. "No one'll come near you!"

"I'm just going to stay with the sweet little lambs," Soppy Susan sniffed.

"Lambs aren't sweet," said Minnie, thinking fast. "They're smelly. And they bite! They've got long pointy teeth like vampires!"

"EEEK!" squealed Susan. "I want to get off! I feel sick!"

"Sick?" said Minnie. "That reminds me..."

She pulled her peashooter from under her beret, together with a small jar of green sludge.

"Mushy peas," grinned Minnie. She poured some cold, mushy, green gloop into her peashooter, took careful aim and...

"SPLAT!"

The first mushy-pea blob went straight up Billy Whizz's nose (which takes a bit of doing at the speed he moves at).

"SQUELCH!"

Mushy peas hit Pie Face in the eye.

"Er – any chance of a pie with that?" Pie Face asked hopefully.

"SPLURGE!"

The last portion hit the back of Mr McDonald's head and covered his bald spot. "That's better than a wig!" chortled Minnie.

Mr McDonald stopped the bus, marched to the back and confiscated the peashooter.

Minnie scowled and looked around the bus as they started off again. Fatty Fudge was already opening his packed lunch. A minxing gleam came into Minnie's eyes. She opened her rucksack and pulled out a chocolate cake. It was large, it was chocolatey, it was covered in icing and... it was completely made out of rubber.

"Perfect!" grinned Minnie. She leaned over and tapped Fatty on the shoulder.

"Are you peckish?" she asked, waving the chocolate cake under his nose.

"Yummy scrummy!" squealed Fatty when he saw the cake. "Gimme gimme!"

He swiped the cake out of Minnie's hands, opened his mouth as wide as he could and CHOMPED!

" *YOWEEEEE!*"

yelled Fatty, as the rubber cake made his jaws spring painfully apart.

"Serves you right, greedy guts!" chortled Minnie as the bus screeched to a halt again. Mr McDonald stormed up to the back, grabbed the cake and glared at Minnie.

"No more minxing!" he bellowed. "Or I'll send you home!"

"Good!" retorted Minnie.

By the time they arrived at the farm, the bus was a bit the worse for wear.

The curtains were hanging off the rails.

Mushy peas had covered most of the seats – and the people in them.

Half the class needed plasters and bandages. The other half was dripping wet (Minnie had brought her water bombs with her).

The lady farmer was standing by the farm gate, waiting for them. She waved as the class limped off the bus.

"Welcome to my farm!" she giggled. "My name is Fifi. You can call me Farmer Fifi!"

"What do you say?" asked Mr McDonald.

"Yuck!" Minnie replied.

"What do you say?" roared Mr McDonald.

"Good morning, Farmer Fifi," muttered the class.

"I love farming," simpered Farmer Fifi. "And I love little children. So we're going to have lots of fun today!"

Minnie stuck her fingers down her throat and Mr McDonald glared at her.

"Any questions before we start?"

"Do you have a dairy?" asked Fatty Fudge.

"Yes," smiled Farmer Fifi.

"With cream and milk and cheese?" asked Fatty Fudge.

"Yes," said Farmer Fifi.

There was a loud rumbling sound from Fatty's stomach.

"Follow me, children!" Farmer Fifi skipped off into the farm and the class followed reluctantly.

First she led them into the barn. A flock of sheep was huddled in the corner.

"It's shearing time," explained Farmer Fifi. "But my farmhand is off sick at the moment, so the sheep will have to wait until he gets back."

She pointed at the shearing machine and then clapped her hands together.

"Let's move along, shall we dears?" said Farmer Fifi.

The class trooped out after Farmer Fifi. But Minnie hung behind and stayed in the barn. Those sheep looked really hot. And she had just had one of her brilliant ideas.

Minnie picked up the shearing machine. She looked at the sheep excitedly.

The sheep looked at Minnie nervously. They started to back away.

"This is gonna be awesome," said Minnie.

Ten minutes later, the barn looked like it had been it by a snowstorm.

There was wool on the ground and wool on the walls. There was wool floating in the air. There was wool in Minnie's hair and wool in her shoes.

There wasn't much wool left on the sheep.

"Wicked," said Minnie, looking at her creations.

"Minnie, don't lag behind," called Mr McDonald's voice.

"My sheep!"
screamed Farmer Fifi.
There were sheep with crew cuts

and sheep with mohicans. There were sheep with bobs and sheep with mullets. There were even a couple of sheep with bunches.

Mr McDonald opened his mouth, but no sound came out.

The sheep were admiring their reflections in an old tin bath in the corner. Minnie gave a smirk.

"I think they look awesome," she chuckled as Farmer Fifi staggered into the barn. "Anyway, I couldn't help it. They kept moving!"

"My wool!" Farmer Fifi gasped. "I can't sell it like that!"

"Hmm, serve you right for never giving them funky haircuts," retorted Minnie.

"You little minx!" yelled Farmer Fifi. "How can I exhibit my sheep at the county show? They all look like punk rock stars! I'll be the laughing stock of the Jolly Farmers Club!

"Did someone say something about a dairy?" asked Fatty Fudge hopefully.

"NO!" bellowed Mr McDonald. He hauled Minnie out of the barn and waggled his finger in her face.

"You are not to shear anything else! And you are not to say another word until I say so! Do you hear me?"

His face was starting to go purple and a minxing grin spread across Minnie's face. She nodded and drew a pretend zip across her mouth.

"Now, children," said Farmer Fifi, trying to calm down (and to forget about her punk-rock sheep). "I have a treat for you next."

"The dairy?" asked Fatty Fudge.

"No, the horses!" smiled Farmer Fifi. "I'm sure that all the little girls will be especially excited. Little girls love ponies!"

"Hmmm, that depends on the

pony," grinned Minnie to herself.

"Oo-er, I hope they don't nip!" quivered Soppy Susan.

The class followed Farmer Fifi over to the stables. There were several horses lined up in a row. Soppy Susan gave a squeal of excitement.

"Oh, they're so cute!" she gushed, rushing up to a white pony with pink bows in its mane.

"That's my favourite pony," simpered Farmer Fifi. "She's called Sweetums."

"Yuck," thought Minnie. "Who'd want a soppy pony like that?"

Just then the horse next to the white pony swished its tail and hit Soppy Susan around the back of the head.

52

"Yes, well, perhaps you had better steer clear of Nipper," said Farmer Fifi, as Soppy Susan let out a loud wail. Nipper curled back his lips and rolled his eyes. Soppy Susan almost fainted.

"That's my kinda pony," grinned Minnie.

"Everyone, get onto a pony!" called Farmer Fifi. "We will have a nice, safe walk in a little circle. Nothing scary!"

"Hmmm, we'll see about that," thought Minnie. She swung herself up onto Nipper's back. Soppy Susan sat on Sweetums. Fatty Fudge's pony kept backing away from him and Plug sat on his pony backwards. Mr McDonald took several deep breaths.

53

"Now, everyone, we're going to walk in a circle," called Farmer Fifi. "Don't be scared, children! Just remember, whatever you do, don't dig your heels in."

Nipper was already going faster than the other ponies, trying to reach Sweetums and give her a nip. Minnie stuck one finger in her ear and jiggled it around.

"Hmm, I've suddenly gone a bit deaf," she chortled. I think Farmer Fifi just told us to dig our heels in. She dug her bony heels into Nipper's sides.

"NEIGGHHH!"

whinnied Nipper. He shot out of the circle of ponies, over the fence and into the field next to the stables. Farmer Fifi clutched her hair.

"NO!" she cried. "My turnips!
"STOP!"

54

Minnie held tight to the reins as Nipper charged across the field, crushing rows of turnips beneath his hooves. He leapt across the next fence.

"My cornfield!" burbled Farmer Fifi. "Just shout 'WHOA!', you wretched minx!"

Nipper sailed through three more fields, pounding through newly planted crops and over freshly turned earth.

"Weeks of work!" screeched Farmer Fifi. "WHOA, Nipper! WHOA!"

The class watched open-mouthed as Nipper charged through the last field and trotted back to the stables. Minnie grinned as she jumped down.

"Why didn't you shout 'WHOA'?" seethed Mr McDonald.

"But sir, you told me not to say another word," said Minnie, opening her eyes wide. "So how could I shout 'WHOA'? I was just doing as I was told, sir. Being a good girl, sir."

Mr McDonald narrowed his eyes and glared at Minnie. But Farmer Fifi gave a weak smile.

"The little girl obviously didn't realise she was doing something wrong," she said.

"I wouldn't bet on it," said Mr McDonald through gritted teeth.

The cowshed was the next stop.

"Now, everyone, I want you to pick some grass to feed to the cows," said Farmer Fifi. The class wandered over to a patch of grass and started picking.

"I've got a nice juicy dandelion for them," said Soppy Susan.

"Do they like buttercups?" asked Plug.

Minnie shook her head. She had several handfuls of grass and little white plants.

"These are their favourites," she said, handing the plants around. "Never mind soppy old dandelions."

The class hurried into the milking shed and started to feed the cows, who munched happily on the grass and plants. Minnie chuckled to herself. Just as Soppy Susan was feeding her cow, Farmer Fifi walked past her and gave a shriek.

"What are you doing, girl?"

"Feeding the cows, Miss," said Soppy Susan.

"With wild garlic?" cried Farmer Fifi. "That stuff smells terrible! Nobody will be able to drink their milk for days!"

"But Minnie said they liked it!" sobbed Soppy Susan.

"MINNIE!"

roared Mr McDonald.

Farmer Fifi had a very bad day.

Actually, it was the very worst day she had ever had.

She was even starting to change her mind about little children.

Fatty Fudge mysteriously tumbled into the pigsty as Minnie walked past him.

The door to the goat shed somehow swung open and the goats chewed Soppy Susan's clothes.

Minnie was helping Plug look at his reflection in the duck pond when he fell in and scared all the ducks.

By the time they had pulled Plug out of the pond and removed three goldfish from his left ear, Farmer Fifi's hair was standing on end. Her eyes were wide and her clothes were dishevelled (the goats had nibbled those as well).

"You... you... LEAVE, she burbled, pointing at the school bus.

"What about the dairy?" asked Fatty Fudge.

"OUT!" screeched Farmer Fifi. "I'm banning children from my farm! OUT!"

The bruised, battered and dishevelled class raced gladly onto the bus. Mr McDonald started the engine and the bus roared away from the farm.

Minnie turned around and watched the figure of Farmer Fifi getting smaller and smaller in the distance. She was shaking a fist as they turned the corner. Minnie looked at Fatty Fudge, who was still covered in pigsty manure. She looked at Soppy Susan's best clothes, which were chewed to ribbons. She looked at Plug, who had just found another goldfish up his left nostril. Minnie gave a wide, wide smile.

"You know, Dad was right, that was fun." she chuckled. "It turns out that Mother Nature is a minx too!"

PIRATE PEST

"I can't believe it!" whooped Dad. "The boss's yacht for an entire weekend!"

He gave a loud cheer and rubbed his hands together. Mum was upstairs, packing and singing something about being a millionaire.

Minnie folded her arms, stuck out her lip and frowned so hard that her eyebrows joined together.

"But I don't want to spend the weekend on a yacht," she fumed. "I'll miss two whole days of minxing!"

"And why is that a bad thing?" asked Dad.

Before Minnie could think of a retort, there was a loud thumping sound as Mum ran downstairs.

"I'm just popping next door to boast – er – I mean – to tell them about the yacht!" she called.

"Show off," muttered Minnie under her breath.

Chester, the family cat, gave a loud hiss. For once, he agreed with Minnie. He didn't like the sound of the yacht. Yachts meant water, and water meant getting wet (especially when Minnie was around). Chester gave another hiss and tried to think of a way to escape.

It was no use. Minnie bellowed and Chester hissed, but they were shoved into the car first thing on Saturday morning and Dad set off for the harbour.

"I'm going to sunbathe on deck!" giggled Mum. "I've got a new bikini for the occasion! You could join me, Minnie!"

Minnie scowled. "I'd rather spend the weekend with Soppy Susan," she said. "There's no way I'm getting into a bikini!"

"I've told everyone that we're spending the weekend on a yacht!" said Mum. "They're all so jealous!"

"They're welcome to it," said Minnie. "Boring, boring, boring."

But Mum wasn't listening. She was dreaming of the gleaming white yacht, blue skies and sparkling champagne.

Mum was in for a shock.

When they arrived at the harbour, Dad got out a scrap of paper.

"It's mooring number BARM13," he said.

Mum dashed past the rows of sleek yachts. "Which one will it be?" she cried in excitement. Minnie followed crossly, dragging her heels.

Suddenly Mum stopped. Her face went white.

"Did you say BARM13?' she asked, through gritted teeth.

"That's right!" grinned Dad. "Is she a beauty?"

Mum just pointed. The only boat at that mooring was old, faded and about half the size of the others around it.

Minnie felt a lot happier.

"Awesome!" she chortled. "That leaky old tub looks like it was around at Trafalgar! It's bound to sink and we'll be stranded on a desert island! Brilliant!"

She leapt on board as Mum glared at Dad. He gave a nervous smile.

"It's still a boat," he said.

"Only just," Mum seethed as she followed Minnie on board.

Soon the boat was chugging out of the harbour to the open sea. Dad was at the controls, wearing a captain's hat. Mum had decided to make the best of it and was lying on the deck in her bikini, covered in goosebumps and trying to pretend she was at the French Riviera. Chester had dug his claws in to the wooden deck and was clinging on for dear life.

"Dad, can I drive the boat?" Minnie asked for the thirteenth time in five minutes.

"No, me hearty, that's a job for Cap'n Dad!" he replied.

"You're being daft," Minnie growled at him.

"I'm just returning to my roots!" Dad cried. "Salt water runs in my veins! I come from a long line of seafarers! This is where I belong!

Pull up the anchors and away, me hearties!"

Minnie gave a groan. This was going to be a long day.

Dad steered towards Gull Island, which was just a little dot on the horizon. Minnie wondered if she could launch the emergency raft and paddle back to land, when suddenly Mum gave a moan.

"I don't feel very well!" she said.

"You've gone a very funny shade of green!" said Minnie, interestedly.

"Ugh! I feel a bit poorly too!" said Dad. "I think I'm going to be—"

"SICK!" cried Mum. Together she and Dad raced down into the cabin and fought to get to the toilet first.

"Hmm," said Minnie. "Looks like there's only one thing for it. PIRATE MINNIE TAKES THE YACHT!"

She made sure the yacht was still heading for Gull Island, then turned to look at her boat.

"Captured fair and square!" she grinned, as Chester tried to scurry down to the cabin. "Oh no you don't, my lad. It's the mast for you, sonny!"

She grabbed Chester by the collar and used a piece of old rope to tie him to the mast.

"That'll stop you falling in the sea," she told him. "And it makes you the last member of the crew to be captured by Pirate Minnie!"

Minnie took the boat further out to sea without any problems at all.

"Har har, dad was right!" she gloated. "But I'm the natural sailor in the family!"

Suddenly she spotted movement a little way ahead. It was a tiny dinghy and there were two women and a man inside, waving frantically at Minnie. She drew up alongside them.

71

"Thank goodness!" exclaimed the man. "Our motor has broken down and we can't get back to land!"

"And what do you want Pirate Minnie to do about it?" asked Minnie in her best piratical drawl.

"Er, well," stammered the man, feeling slightly alarmed. "If you could get us back to shore..."

"Throw me a rope," said Minnie. The man threw her a rope and she secured it to the back of the yacht. "I'll give you a tow," said Minnie.

"Oh, I say," sniffed one of the women. "Couldn't you let us on board?"

"Not on your nelly!" Minnie declared. "I'm Pirate Minnie and I know all the tricks of the high seas!"

She marched to the front of the yacht and set off again. "Full speed ahead!"

The yacht powered off across the waves, dragging the little dinghy behind it. The three passengers bounced up and down over the waves.

"I say!" shouted the man. "We're feeling a bit sick back here!"

"Landlubbers!" roared Pirate Minnie. Then her attention was grabbed by something sticking out of the water. Something that was getting taller and taller...

"A periscope!" Minnie cried. "Awesome! That means a submarine!"

Minnie stopped the yacht again and held her position next to the periscope. The periscope turned slowly to face her and Minnie whipped her catapult out from

under her beret. She squinted, closed
one eye, aimed and shot a dried pea
straight down the periscope.

"SHOT!" she yelled, punching the
air and leaping around the yacht.

The pea zoomed into the
periscope, rattled down the funnel
and PINGED into the first
lieutenant's eye.

" *YOWEEEEE!*"

he yelled, staggering
out of the conning
tower and onto the
bridge. He collided
with the officer of the
watch, who stumbled

backwards and landed on a large, red button labelled 'Do not push!'

Alarms began to sound and red lights started to flash all over the submarine. "The torpedo launcher!" yelled the Captain. "Stop the launch!" He clutched at his hair and pulled a couple of clumps out.

"Torpedo away!" announced torpedo control over the intercom.

The torpedo zoomed through the water towards Gull Island as the Captain collapsed into a chair and a sub-lieutenant fanned him with a map of Wales.

Minnie heard a dull thump as the torpedo hit the island and then saw a plume of water burst into the air. Seagulls shot into the air in terror, scattering droppings across the island.

"Dive for cover!" yelled one of the men on the beach. "We're being bombed!"

The sunbathers threw towels over their heads and raced for the shelter of the trees, as they were caught in a hail of white droppings.

"Brilliant!" Minnie sniggered as the periscope started to rise up out of the water. "Uh-oh – time to make tracks!"

She powered the yacht away from Gull Island and the submarine. The little dinghy bobbed along behind her. All three of its passengers were hanging over the sides, their faces green.

Minnie darted down to the cabin and grabbed an old white sheet. She passed Mum and Dad, who were lying in their bunks and groaning. She passed a metal detector leaning against the cabin door.

"That might come in handy!" Minnie said to herself.

She grabbed a fat marker pen and drew a skull and crossbones on the sheet. Then she raced up to the deck and attached the sheet to the mast, just as the submarine surfaced.

"The Jolly Roger!" she whooped. "No one stops Pirate Minnie!"

"PIRATES!" screamed the naval officers as they peered out of the submarine. "Help!"

Minnie steered the boat away as the officers clutched each other in terror.

"Time for a speedy escape!" she told Chester, who glared at her and gave a loud hiss.

Minnie raced over the waves, which were getting quite choppy, ignoring the weak cries of the people in the dinghy. She sped into the harbour and scraped the yacht along the side of the harbour wall with a loud

SCREEEECH.

Minnie pointed the yacht at the mooring bay, nudged a couple of sleek white boats out of the way and came to a full stop.

"Land ahoy, me hearties!" she bellowed.

There were loud groans from the cabin and Mum and Dad staggered onto dry land.

Minnie untied Chester and he sprang off the boat and up the walkway to the car.

The people in the dinghy paddled around to the landing stage and heaved themselves onto the walkway. They stayed lying there, motionless and green. Mum and Dad sat down and clutched each other.

"This has been a great day for pirating!" Minnie said as she looked at her captives.

"You – little – minx!" choked Dad, still fighting down the urge to be sick.

"Just you wait until I can stand!" added Mum, whose legs were feeling very rubbery.

"I think it's about time to leave!" chortled Minnie. She grabbed the metal detector she had spotted earlier and charged up the walkway and away from the harbour, heading for the beach.

"That's where all the treasure'll be buried!" she chuckled.

Minnie turned on the detector and started to sweep it across the sand, listening to the clicks, beeps and whirrs through the headphones.

At first there didn't seem to be much treasure.

BEEP! BEEP!

A tin whistle.

BEEP! BEEP!

An old fork with two of its prongs missing.

BEEP! BEEP!

A medal for 'Beanotown's Sweetest Girl 1962'.

But then the metal detector started to beep really loudly. As Minnie walked closer to the shoreline, the beeps grew even louder and more excited.

"This must be some real pirate booty!" Minnie said in delight. "I'll be rich! I'll buy the sweetshop! And the joke shop! And I'll send Dennis the Menace to Australia!"

Minnie started to dig at the shoreline, sure that soon she would uncover a treasure chest.

She didn't notice a periscope breaking the water in front of her.

She didn't notice the grey metal of a submarine rising out of the sea.

The metal detector went crazy. It had detected the submarine!

"I'm nearly there!" cried Minnie, digging even faster. Suddenly she heard splashes and shouts. She looked up. Five naval officers had jumped out of the submarine and were wading through the waves towards her.

"Time to scarper!" cried Minnie. She dropped the metal detector, flung the headphones on the sand and sped up the beach towards the harbour car park. Mum and Dad were sitting in the car, still looking a bit green around the gills.

"Come back here you little minx!" yelled the Captain, emptying sand out of his shoes.

"Stop!" hollered the first lieutenant, pulling a crab off his nose.

"Help!" gurgled the officer of the watch, as a piece of stringy seaweed went up his nose. (He didn't really like the sea and had only joined the navy because his mumsy told him to).

Minnie reached the car and jumped in, landing on Chester.

"YOWL!" Chester caterwauled.

"DRIVE!" bellowed Minnie. "Go, Dad, go!"

Dad hit the accelerator and they sped off. Behind them, the harbour master, the people from the dinghy and the three officers waved their fists and yelled. Minnie leaned back with a happy sigh.

"What a great day!" she grinned. "I thought I'd miss out on minxing, but it turns out that pirates are the best minxes of all!"

Mum turned around and glared at her.

"I'm glad you like pirates," she said, "because as soon as we get home, I've got a very piratical treat for you."

"What's that?" asked Minnie in excitement.

"You're going to be walking the plank," said Mum. "STRAIGHT INTO THE BATH!"

"NO!" hollered Minnie. "I'm trapped! I feel sick! Let me out!"

"Not likely," said Dad with a grin. "You're our captive now!"

"That's the last time I play

pirates!" Minnie humphed. "I wasn't seasick, but I am TOTALLY sick of the sea!"

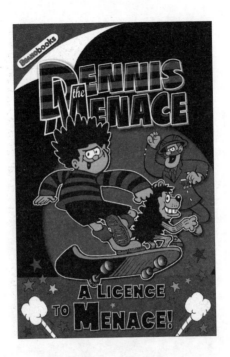

Written by RACHEL ELLIOT

Illustrated by BARRIE APPLEBY

published under licence by

meadowside
CHILDREN'S BOOKS

185 Fleet Street, London, EC4A 2HS

www.meadowsidebooks.com

Printed and bound in Great Britain by William Clowes Ltd, Beccles, Suffolk

10 9 8 7 6 5 4 3 2 1